Dora Saves Crystal Kingdom

Adapted by Mary Tillworth
Based on a screenplay by Chris Gifford
Illustrated by Dave Aikins

Random House 🏠 New York

randomhouse.com/kids
ISBN: 978-0-449-81450-5
MANUFACTURED IN CHINA   10 9 8 7 6 5 4 3 2 1

Dora and Boots were enjoying a beautiful day outside. Boots wanted to listen to a story, so Dora found a book called *The Crystal Kingdom*. Dora and Boots settled down to read the tale together.

Once upon a time, there were four magic crystals that brought color to the Crystal Kingdom. They were yellow, green, blue, and red. When they joined together, they made a beautiful rainbow. The townspeople loved their colorful world.

One day, a greedy king used his magic wand to take all the crystals for himself. Without the crystals, the town lost its wonderful color! The king hid the crystals in other stories, where no one could find them.

A brave girl named Allie wanted to rescue the crystals. She searched all over, but they were nowhere to be found.

Suddenly, Dora's crystal necklace started flashing! It shined a rainbow that ended at the kingdom where Allie lived!

Allie flew out of her story and appeared before Dora and Boots. She asked them to help her find the crystals. Dora and Boots jumped into the book with Allie.

Dora checked Map for directions. Map said the yellow crystal was in *The Dragon Land Story*, the green one was in *The Butterfly Cave Story*, the blue one was in *The Magic Castle Story*, and the red one was in *The Crystal Kingdom Story*.

"Let's go to the first story! *¡La primera historia!*" said Dora, and off they went.

Dora and Boots landed in *The Dragon Land Story*! They found a knight who was fighting a dragon, but the dragon was friendly.

Dora thought quickly. She used a rope from Backpack to lasso the sword so the knight and the dragon would stop fighting.

The knight and the dragon were glad to become friends. And the dragon knew where the yellow crystal was hidden! He had seen the king put it inside a cliff. The dragon flew Dora, Boots, Allie, and the knight to the cliff.

With his fire breath, the dragon blasted the cliff open to show the yellow crystal. But the king tried to steal it with his magic wand! The knight raised her shield and blocked his spell.

Now Dora had the yellow crystal! The knight gave Dora the shield to help her on the quest. Next, Dora needed to find the green crystal in *The Butterfly Cave Story.*

"¡La segunda historia!" she said.

Everyone made it to the Butterfly Cave in the second story! The green crystal was inside the twelfth cocoon. Dora and Boots counted to twelve and found the crystal!

Butterflies hatched from the cocoons and gave everyone a pair of magic butterfly wings. Now Dora and Boots had to find the blue crystal in *The Magic Castle Story*.

"¡La tercera historia!" said Dora to get into the third story.

In the Magic Castle, Dora and Boots met a magician named Enrique. The blue crystal was hidden in his hat.

"Abracadabra!" said Dora, and she got the crystal.

To help her on her way, Enrique gave Dora his magic wand. Now, to save the Crystal Kingdom, all Dora needed was the red crystal!

To get into the last story, Dora said, *"¡La cuarta historia!"*

Dora and Boots were in *The Crystal Kingdom Story*! The greedy king had put the red crystal in his crown. Dora and Boots used their butterfly wings to reach him.

The king cast a spell and sent rocks flying through the air. But Dora and Boots blocked the rocks with the shield the knight had given them.

The king used his magic wand to cast a spell on Dora, but Dora had a magic wand, too. She blocked the magic, flew up to the king, and got the red crystal!

"The crystals are for everyone to share," Dora told the greedy king. He realized she was right.

With all the crystals back, the color returned to Crystal Kingdom! The king was surprised when he saw everyone sharing the crystals. He saw that they were happy, and he wanted to share and be happy, too. The king gave Allie his crown and made her the queen. *¡La reina!*

The town threw a party to celebrate the return of the crystals! Dora and Boots knew they couldn't have gotten the crystals back without the help of all their brave friends.

Thanks to Dora and Boots, Unicornio was a kind and fair king once again.
All the forest creatures lived happily ever after.

King Unicornio told Owl to invite everyone to a party in the Enchanted Forest. At the celebration, all the forest creatures cheered, "*¡Viva el rey Unicornio!* Long live King Unicornio!"

The elves fixed the dam! Unicornio was free! Dora, Boots, and Unicornio soon found Owl.

"Owl, you are very smart, but you must learn to get along with others and treat everyone fairly," Unicornio said.

Owl realized that Unicornio was right, and he returned the crown.

"Tell the elves to bring their tools!" Dora called to Rabbit as he hopped away. "¡Rápido!"

Quick as a flash, the elves arrived with their tools. They were eager to fix the dam so that Unicornio could be king of the Enchanted Forest again.

Dora and Boots found Unicornio at the dam. They had to save him!
Dora and Boots remembered that the elves were really good at fixing
things, so they sent Rabbit to get them.

At the Fairy Tunnel, Dora and Boots asked the fairies to light the way.
Just then, Owl showed up and had his mini-owls blow out the fairies' lights!
But one little fairy still had her light. With her help, Dora and Boots made
it through the Fairy Tunnel and into the Enchanted Forest!

The elves saw that Dora and Boots needed help. Working together, they fixed the bridge and ran across to the Elf Garden.

"*Muchas gracias,*" Dora told the elves. "Now on to the Fairy Tunnel!"

Dora and Boots raced down the path to the Elf Garden and came to a bridge. Suddenly, Owl flew by. He told the mini-owls to take the screws out of the bridge so Dora and Boots couldn't cross it!

With Scarecrow's help, Dora and Boots called a flock of crows to pick up the corn. Soon the crows had cleared the path so Dora and Boots could head to their next stop—the Elf Garden!

Before Scarecrow could answer, Owl flew by. He didn't want Dora to help save King Unicornio. He told his mini-owls to pile up lots of corn to block the path to the Enchanted Forest!

Dora and Boots headed down the path to get to the Cornfield. There they saw a scarecrow perched on his pole.

"¡Hola, Scarecrow!" Dora called. "Can we get through the Cornfield, por favor?"

"We've got to hurry to the Enchanted Forest," Boots said.
"Map can help us!" Dora declared.
Map showed the way. To reach the forest, Dora and Boots had to go
through the Cornfield, past the Elf Garden, and through the Fairy Tunnel.

Now all the forest creatures had to follow Owl's rules! They were very unhappy. There was only one person who could help them. Dora!

Rabbit found Dora and Boots outside Dora's house.

"¡Vengan rapido!" Rabbit said. "We've got to rescue Unicornio so he can be king of the Enchanted Forest again!"

Owl was not like King Unicornio. Instead of letting the forest creatures roam free, he made new, unfair rules.

When the king returned, Owl did not want to give the crown back. He ordered his mini-owls to make a crack in a dam. If King Unicornio didn't plug the crack, the Enchanted Forest would flood. Owl trapped Unicornio there and flew off with the crown.

Once upon a time, the wise and brave Unicornio was crowned king of the Enchanted Forest. He was a kind and fair king, and all the forest creatures were happy.

Then one day the king needed to help some friends outside the Enchanted Forest. He gave his crown to Owl and asked him to watch over the kingdom.

Adapted by Mary Tillworth

Based on the screenplay
"Dora Saves King Unicornio" by Rosemary Contreras

Illustrated by Victoria Miller

Random House 🏠 New York

© 2011, 2013 Viacom International Inc. All rights reserved. Published in the United States by Random House Children's Books,
a division of Random House, Inc., 1745 Broadway, New York, NY 10019, and in Canada by Random House of Canada Limited, Toronto.
Originally published in slightly different form by Simon & Schuster, Inc., in 2011. Random House and the colophon
are registered trademarks of Random House, Inc. Nickelodeon, Dora the Explorer, and all related titles, logos,
and characters are trademarks of Viacom International Inc.
randomhouse.com/kids
ISBN: 978-0-449-81450-5
MANUFACTURED IN CHINA   10 9 8 7 6 5 4 3 2 1